MICH.

SIDE SPLITTING
STORIES

By Matthew K. Manning
Illustrated by Ethen Beavers

STONE ARCH BOOKS
a capstone imprint

Michael Dahl Presents is published by Stone Arch Books,
an imprint of Capstone.
1710 Roe Crest Drive
North Mankato, Minnesota 56003
www.capstonepub.com

Library of Congress Cataloging-in-Publication Data
Names: Manning, Matthew K., author.
Title: Bug brigade / Matthew K. Manning.
Description: North Mankato, MN : Stone Arch Books, [2020] | Series: Michael
    Dahl presents: Side-splitting stories | Audience: Ages 8-12. | Audience:
    Grades 4-6. | Summary: Proud members of the Bug Society of Littleton,
    sixth-graders Doug, Josie, Kira, and Reginald, are transformed into
    part-insect superheroes when they get mixed up with a mad scientist's
    experiment involving radioactive bugs—and they have to use their insect
    superpowers to defeat the evil insect villain.
Identifiers: LCCN 2019039625 (print) | LCCN 2019039626 (ebook) | ISBN
    9781496587039 (hardcover) | ISBN 9781496592071 (paperback) | ISBN
    9781496587084 (eBook pdf)
Subjects: LCSH: Insects—Juvenile fiction. | Superheroes—Juvenile fiction.
    | Supervillains—Juvenile fiction. | Science—Experiments—Juvenile
    fiction. | Mutation (Biology)—Juvenile fiction. | Humorous stories. |
    CYAC: Insects—Fiction. | Superheroes—Fiction. |
    Supervillains—Fiction. | Science—Experiments—Fiction. | Humorous
    stories. | LCGFT: Superhero fiction. | Humorous fiction.
Classification: LCC PZ7.M315614 Bu 2020 (print) | LCC PZ7.M315614 (ebook)
    | DDC 813.6 [Fic]—dc23
LC record available at https://lccn.loc.gov/2019039625
LC ebook record available at https://lccn.loc.gov/2019039626

Designer: Hilary Wacholz

MICHAEL
DAHL
PRESENTS

Michael Dahl has written about werewolves, magicians, and superheroes. He loves funny books, scary books, and mysterious books. Every Michael Dahl Presents book is chosen by Michael himself and written by an author he loves. The books are about favorite subjects like monster aliens, haunted houses, farting pigs, or magical powers that go haywire. Read on!

TABLE OF CONTENTS

A "LAFFY" LAUGH!

When I was in middle school, my friends recorded me laughing. (They did it in secret.) I guess my laugh sounded so goofy that it made them laugh too. My friends were pretty funny themselves. They told great jokes and hilarious stories. I wish I had written them down. But that gave me the idea to have some of my new friends write down their stories. If you feel a chuckle or a guffaw deep inside while reading, let it out. Who knows—maybe your laugh will end up in a video!

Michael Dahl

CHAPTER 1

THE DOWNSIDE OF HIDING UNDER A DESK

Okay, I'll admit it. I wasn't supposed to be there. Honestly, I wasn't even supposed to be in that building. I should have been with the rest of my sixth grade class in the main hall of the Blue Mountain Science Museum.

It should have been your standard, run-of-the-mill field trip full of bored faces and plenty of yawns. I was definitely not supposed to be hiding under a desk with my friends Kira, Reginald, and Josie in a top-secret, off-limits laboratory. Because if I had been where I should have been, I wouldn't now be staring at a crazy-looking scientist in a white lab coat holding a vial of glowing orange liquid and ranting to himself.

"I don't give a horse's patoot what the board says!" said the man in the white lab coat. He stormed across the room.

I was the only one who could really see him from where we were. There, under the desk, I was closest to the wall. The small gap between the wall and the desk meant I had a pretty good view of the strange man in front of me. I looked back at my friends.

"Patoot?" I mouthed.

Kira shrugged. She didn't know what it meant either. So I turned back to the gap.

The man in the white lab coat ran his fingers through his thin black hair. He seemed nervous. "You know what? I'm just going to do it," he said. He pulled a tank full of insects closer to him. There was a label on its side. It was hard to make out, but I tried anyway. We had sneaked into this wing of the museum to see the new insect exhibits. I wasn't about to miss my chance to see what kind of rare bugs were squirming around in that tank.

I squinted and read: *Indigenous Insects to the Carolinas.* Then something hopped inside the tank. I couldn't see what it was. I could only tell that the tank was divided into a few dozen sections. It was killing me not to know which particular bugs were in there.

The man in the white lab coat couldn't stop his hands from shaking. He had this weird look on his face. It was like he was trying to convince himself of something. I was pretty sure he was losing whatever argument he was having with himself. Suddenly he raised the vial containing the orange liquid above the tank. He slid open the lid and closed his eyes. Then he sprinkled the glowing liquid over each squared-off section.

I could see the strange glowing orange goo rain down on the insects inside. There was a flurry of flittering wings and twitching legs. Whatever the orange stuff was, the bugs didn't like it. They bumped against the sides of the tank over and over again. And then they got really still. Were they even still alive? I was about to turn to Kira to see what she thought when I heard the buzzing.

It all happened so fast. It was like the bugs were operating with a single hive mind. The man in the white lab coat looked down at them. Suddenly the insects burst out of the open lid.

They were swarming.

The man was screaming.

I scrambled back from the gap between the desk and the wall.

"What is it, Doug?" Kira whispered.

I couldn't answer. I was too shocked. All I could do was shake my head.

I looked back through the gap just in time to see dozens of glowing insects flying directly at us.

CHAPTER 2

THE ABSOLUTE WRONG SIDE OF THE BED

"Ladybugs!" I shouted as I sat up in bed the next morning.

That was certainly a first. I'd been on this planet for eleven years. In that time, I'd woken up in plenty of weird ways. There was the morning when I woke up under my bed. (I'm pretty sure I rolled off my mattress in the middle of the night.) There was the time I fell asleep in the bathtub.

(I don't recommend waking up in a pool of near-freezing water.) I even woke up in the dog's bed once. (Still not sure how that one happened.) But this was the first time I'd ever woken myself up by yelling about ladybugs.

My heart was racing. I wasn't getting back to sleep anytime soon. So I swung my legs off the side of the bed. That's when I felt the pain for the first time. It was coming from right above my left calf.

My legs looked paler than usual, and that's saying something. I pulled my left leg closer to my face. There was a large red bump where I was pretty sure there hadn't been one before. Then the memories came flooding back.

The sixth-grade field trip. The museum's Insect Wing was set to open next month. As Littleton's biggest fans of the bug world, the four of us couldn't wait for the ribbon-cutting ceremony. So we ducked under a barrier, sneaked past a security guard, and headed into the new wing of the building that was still under construction.

And then it had been just like the dream. The man in the white lab coat. Hiding under the desk. Flapping wings and a cloud of bugs. It was chaos, so we took off running as fast as we could back to meet our class. Kira, Reginald, and Josie said they'd been bitten by some of the insects in all the craziness. Until this morning, I thought I'd made it out okay.

I shook my head, got dressed, and walked down the stairs into the kitchen.

"He lives," said Dad. He looked up from his tablet. I didn't have to ask what he was reading. It was the local news. It was always the news. "You hear about this robbery at the food co-op?" he asked.

I didn't answer. I was still trying to get my head around those insects at the museum.

"Somebody broke in and stole a few dozen crates of produce last night," Dad continued. "Can you imagine? Gotta be pretty desperate to make off with a bunch of lettuce."

I shrugged. I had bigger things to worry about than stolen vegetables. I assumed literally every person on the planet had bigger things to worry about than stolen vegetables.

"You hungry?" asked Mom when she walked into the kitchen. "I just bought a new box of granola. It's in the cabinet."

"Thanks," I said.

It was a usual breakfast for a usual Saturday morning. I liked a good healthy start to the day, even if it was sugar-free and pretty bland. It gave me plenty of energy for basketball practice, which was important if I wanted to stay a starter for the team.

But then it hit me—a weird feeling, deep in my gut. "You know what?" I said. "I'll just grab some fast food on the way to the meeting."

"You?" Mom fanned herself with her hand, pretending she was going to faint.

"Oh," Dad said. "Off to hang out with the Bug Buddies?"

"*Society*," I corrected. "The Bug Society of Littleton."

"His *real* friends," said Mom. "The ones he's too embarrassed to tell his basketball team about."

I shot Mom an annoyed look. "I'm not embarrassed," I said.

"Not embarrassed," she said, "but you don't

want your team to know you're secretly one of the smart ones."

And with that, I'd suddenly had enough morning conversation. So I waved bye and walked out the front door.

"Have fun at the Bug Buddies!" Dad called after me.

"You're terrible, Frank," I heard Mom say. I was pretty sure I could hear Dad laughing, but by that point I was already halfway down the block.

CHAPTER 3

NEVER TALK TO A TREE WITH LEGS

"I'm not embarrassed," I mumbled as I walked to the park.

I took another bite of my egg sandwich. It was way too greasy. But today, grease tasted good. I didn't think about that too much. I was busy stewing in my anger. What did Mom know? The Bug Society of Littleton was a secret society. By definition, that meant it had to be a secret.

I swallowed another bite of the Egg Fluffie. I had ordered three of these disgusting things. With extra sausage. By the time I'd reached the edge of the park, I had already wolfed down most of the last one. I was starting to wish I'd ordered four.

The whole time, I kept thinking about what Mom had said. I'm not sure why it bothered me so much. I was into insects, sure. But I was also into basketball. Those two things didn't go together.

Most kids grew out of trying to catch bugs and examine them. Most eventually stopped reading about weird centipedes from the Amazon or the working habits of bees. But that's the stuff I thought about all the time, just like the other members of the Bug Society. I made lists of different kinds of beetles when I was lying in bed at night. I drew butterfly wing patterns in the margins of my notebooks.

The rest of my basketball team dreamed of playing college ball or going pro. I wanted to be an entomologist. But other than Kira, Josie, and Reginald, I doubted anyone in my class even knew what that word meant.

I could be myself when I was with the Bug Society. We had joined up a few years ago. Keeping the group a secret was my idea, even though that seemed to annoy some of the others. We met every Saturday, but I kept my distance from them at school.

I didn't want to, but being on the basketball team meant certain . . . sacrifices. I was tall, so basketball came easy for me. But the other stuff the team talked about—video games, sports cars, ultimate fighting—had never been my thing.

I already had trouble fitting in. Drawing attention to the fact that I'm part of a club that studies insects for fun . . . well, that's just asking for problems. Nobody wants to be mocked in the locker room or teased while running drills.

So I laughed at the jokes and played along. Even if that meant ignoring my real friends at school. Even if they might have hated me for it.

"Psst," interrupted a nearby tree.

I stopped in my tracks. I swallowed the last bite of my strangely delicious and equally terrible egg sandwich. There was no one around. It was dark at the edge of the park. The taller trees shaded the sidewalk and the dew-covered lawn.

If not for the lamppost near me, I wouldn't have been able to see the sticklike five-foot tree in front of me very clearly. I could just make out its slender brown trunk as it stood there in some loose soil about ten feet away.

"Over here!" said the tree.

It was a slender brown *talking* tree, apparently.

"Hello?" I said.

"What's doing?" asked the tree.

"You're a tree," I said.

"It's me," the tree said. "Reginald."

"Reginald isn't a tree." I didn't know what else to say.

Just then, I heard a thumping sound above me. I looked up at the lamppost. Flying on paperlike wings was Kira. She was bumping into the light over and over again.

"Kira?" I said. I barely got the name out, I was so stunned.

"Hey, Doug," she said. She pushed her hair out of her eyes and smiled down at me. Then she bumped back into the light. "Isn't this light awesome?"

I looked back at the talking tree. But it had moved. It was now right in front of my face.

"Ah!" I yelled.

"Ah!" yelled the tree.

I took a step back.

"I mean . . . sorry," said the tree. "Here, hold on a second. Let me see if I can still do this."

The tree stretched. Then two insect-like stick arms popped out of its upper trunk. Two just-as-skinny legs popped out of its lower trunk. Then the whole thing shook and puffed up like an air mattress being inflated. Suddenly a tree wasn't standing in front of me. In its place was my friend and fellow Bug Society member Reginald.

"How are you a tree?!" I yelled. I didn't mean to yell, but it's just how it came out.

"I'm a stick-bug," said Reginald. "A giant walking stick, to be precise. I was just camouflaged like stick-bugs do. So I only looked like a tree."

"How are you a stick-bug?!" I shouted.

"The same way Kira is a wavy-lined emerald moth," said Reginald. He smiled. He looked normal now. He was back to his familiar self: stocky frame, dark-brown skin, short hair. The definitely not-a-tree-now Reginald was even wearing his thick, black glasses. If I hadn't just watched him transform from stick-bug into a human with my own eyes, I wouldn't have believed it.

"What is going on?" I asked.

"I think it's because of the bugs that bit us at the museum," said Josie, who was suddenly standing right next to me.

"Ah!" I yelled again. Josie had come out of nowhere. She was lightning-quick, like a . . .

"Cockroach, if you're wondering," said Josie. "I have cockroach powers now. I'm superfast, and my skin is super tough. Here, punch me." She braced herself.

"I'm not going to punch you," I said.

"Can *I* punch you?" asked Reginald.

"Sure!" said Josie.

"Nobody is punching anybody!" I yelled.

By that point, Kira had landed next to me. I looked at her thin, light-green wings. The light of the lamppost shone through them.

"Have you guys seen that light?" asked Kira. "I think it's my favorite."

"It's just a lamppost," I said.

"Where?" said Josie. She looked up at the light. Her big brown eyes looked even bigger than normal behind her large, circle-framed glasses. Then she began to scream. "AAARGH!" she yelled. "Turn it off! Turn it off!" She dropped the backpack she had slung over her shoulder. It fell to the sidewalk with a thud. Several books and pencils fell out of it, scattering on the ground.

Reginald shrugged. "I guess moths and cockroaches see the world differently," he said.

But I wasn't really listening. I was too busy moving in a rush, collecting all of Josie's things. I used a sweatshirt that had been inside Josie's bag and rolled all her belongings into it with a speed I didn't even know was possible. Josie was the smallest member of the Bug Society. She always carried a pile of books nearly as large as she was. Despite all that, I handed her things back to her in the next instant, in a nice, tightly rolled package.

"Wow," said Josie. "That was fast."

"What kind of bug were you bitten by?" asked Reginald.

I remembered the red bump on my leg. "I . . . I don't know," I said. "I didn't see it."

I was staring at Kira again. I couldn't help it. Her wings almost glowed. Anyone walking by would see them.

"We shouldn't be out in public," I said suddenly.

"Is this more of your secret society nonsense?" said Kira. She seemed annoyed as she glanced back

up at the lamppost. "What is that?" she yelled, as if seeing it for the first time. She flew up to it and began bumping into it more. She smacked her head into the lamp over and over. "So pretty!" she kept saying.

Just then, I heard someone cough. An older woman was walking her dog nearby. She seemed tired, not fully awake yet. She nodded to me halfheartedly as she passed.

"Morning," I said casually. I didn't want to draw any more attention to us.

"Good—" the woman started to say when she noticed the repeated thumping above her. She looked up. Then she promptly fell to the ground unconscious. The poodle looked at her. He seemed to realize she had fainted. Then he stepped onto her back. He settled into her armpit and closed his eyes. Apparently it was naptime for both of them.

Kira landed on the sidewalk again. She held her sore forehead in her hand and looked at the snoring old woman.

"Okay," she said. "I get your point. Secret it is."

CHAPTER 4

NOTHING GOOD IS BORN IN A BASEMENT

"Costumes," Reginald repeated. "Superheroes need costumes."

"We're not superheroes," I said. I shifted my position on the couch. Its leather made a squeaking noise.

Josie stared in my direction. "Did you just . . . ?" she said. She was sitting on the cushion next to me.

"It was the couch!" I said. I reached for the remote and turned the TV louder.

"In local news, Marsh's Grocery was robbed late this morning," said the bored-looking reporter on the screen. "The mystery thief or thieves pilfered an unattended delivery truck behind the store, making off with several bushels of kale."

The reporter's lifeless voice was even more annoying than the couch. I pressed the power button.

"Well, *I'm* a superhero," Reginald was saying. "Super Stick-Bug."

"Oh man," said Josie. "That's awesome. I want to be Super Cockroach!"

"I mean, it's a little close to mine," said Reginald. He looked down at the notepad in his lap. He was doodling something that looked like a costume.

"Okay," said Josie. She was now even more excited. She tucked her short, straight black hair behind her ears and said, "Captain Cockroach!"

"I like it," said Kira.

"But you're not in the military," said Reginald.

"Oh, but the Crunch guy on the cereal box is?" said Josie.

"Touché."

"I want to be Moth Girl," said Kira.

"None of us are superheroes!" I said in a voice louder than I'd meant. I'm pretty sure Reginald's parents could hear me from upstairs. Reginald's house was old. It had pretty thick walls, but the basement wasn't soundproof.

"We were bitten by, like, radioactive bugs or

something," said Reginald. "That's textbook origin story right there."

"They weren't radioactive," I said. I shifted on the couch again. It squeaked.

Josie gave me a dirty look. So I stood up and moved over to the floor next to Kira. She was sitting near the old rug on Reginald's concrete floor.

"You guys ever wonder what that scientist guy was trying to do?" said Reginald. He continued to scribble on his pad.

"Professor Lad," corrected Josie. She leaned forward on the couch. Somehow, the couch stayed silent for her. She shot me an I-told-you-so glare. "I looked him up," she said. "Apparently, Lad was just fired from the museum today. He was caught performing 'illegal experiments' on his specimens."

"And we saw it happen!" said Reginald. "How cool is that! I mean, until all the biting and stuff."

"At least you guys know what bit you," I said. "You all have crazy powers. So far, I'm just me."

"And with crazy powers come crazy costumes," said Reginald.

"That's not the saying," said Josie.

I was still tired. That museum trip really had taken a lot out of me. I leaned back against the wall and closed my eyes. When I opened them again, everybody was staring at me.

"What?" I said.

"Dude!" yelled Reginald. "Can you, you know, let me out now?"

Without realizing it, I had rolled Reginald up in the rug. I didn't even know I'd been moving, let alone turning my friend into the human version of a pig in a blanket.

"Guys, don't you get it?" said Josie. She hopped off the couch. The couch remained silent, just to spite me. "Now we know what kind of bug bit Doug!"

I had come to the same conclusion as my friends. I was developing traits that resembled those of an . . . interesting insect.

While I wasn't craving exactly the same "food" as the bug in question, I couldn't shake my hunger for terrible, terrible fast food. And I'd also developed an impressive quick-rolling ability, even if I wasn't rolling the substance this bug was named for.

I didn't want anyone to say it out loud.

To say it out loud would mean it was true.

Josie's grin widened. "A dung beetle!"

She had said it out loud.

CHAPTER 5

SOME THINGS ARE BETTER OFF IN THE BACK OF THE CLOSET

The sweatpants were way too loose on me but somehow way too small at the same time. Nearly half my legs stuck out of the bottom of the pants. Yet the elastic waistband felt like it was barely holding on.

The pants were all Reginald had in his closet that came close to fitting me. So they'd have to do. At least they matched the way-too-loose black sweatshirt I was wearing and the way-too-small knit hat on my head.

"So," said Kira. She had fashioned an impressive gown-like hooded costume out of an old green bedsheet she'd found in Reginald's basement. "What's your superhero name going to be?"

I straightened my back for dramatic effect. I wanted to get this just right. "The Dark Beetle!" I announced.

"Nope," said Reginald. "Not working for me. You're the Doug Beetle."

"That's perfect!" said Kira.

"That's not perfect!" I protested. "It gives away my secret identity. Plus, it doesn't sound the least bit cool."

"You and your secrets," said Kira sarcastically.

"It'd be so awful if people knew what you were really like."

"So it's settled," said Josie, appearing out of nowhere. "You're the Doug Beetle."

"It's not settled!" I argued. "It's not settled at—"

"Shh," interrupted Reginald. He was wearing a yellow tracksuit and an almost-matching yellow mask. He had found the mask in a Halloween costume bin in his basement's closet. It probably should have stayed there. "I'm getting something on the crime tracker."

"Crime tracker?" I said. I had no idea what he was talking about.

I walked over to the corner of the basement and looked at Reginald's laptop.

"Crime tracker, social media," said Reginald. "Same thing."

The video on Reginald's screen belonged to a guy on my basketball team. His name was Leonard, but we all called him L-Bow. (He used his elbows like weapons on the court.)

Reginald pressed play.

"Some dude in a crazy costume is going crazy at the farmers' market!" L-Bow shouted before adding, "Crazy!"

L-Bow was hiding behind a picnic table. In the background was a blurry man in a red and black costume. The man was throwing apples at a group of frightened shoppers. The video ended.

"I think I've found our first case," said Reginald.

"Case?" said Josie. She was suddenly standing right next to me.

"I'm never going to get used to that," I said.

Josie ignored me. She was wearing goggles in place of her glasses. She had on a pair of brown overalls that she had found in Reginald's garage, with a white tank top underneath. Even though Josie had rolled up the legs quite a bit, the overalls fit her even worse than my sweatpants fit me.

At least Josie could still wear her own brown boots with her "costume." It didn't make her homemade antennae headband look any less silly, though.

"The farmers' market is only a few blocks from here," Josie said, looking at each of us. "Race ya!"

I watched as Josie sped out of the basement.

A few seconds later, I could hear Reginald's front door open and slam shut.

Kira, Reginald, and I all looked at one another. Then we ran after Josie. It was too late to back out now. Apparently, we were actually going to give this superhero thing a shot.

CHAPTER 6

APPLES HURT MORE THAN YOU'D THINK

"How does he have so many apples?!" I yelled. I ducked around the corner of the largest red barn at the farmers' market.

Just then, a rotten Granny Smith hit the corner of the barn. Apple pulp flew into my eye. "Ah!" I yelped. It didn't sound very heroic.

"I'm starting to think that's not a costume!" yelled Josie as she sped over toward me. "That guy has fully formed red elytra with black spots!"

It was just like Josie to be perfectly scientific about insect parts in the heat of battle.

"He's a mutated ladybug. I think we should call him LadyBugManGuy," Josie said.

"That's perfect!" said a nearby tree. Then the tree contorted and inflated, revealing Reginald. When back in human form, Reginald was wearing his yellow superhero outfit.

"That's not perfect," I said. "Why do you always think the first name people come up with is—" But I didn't have time to finish the question. I had accidentally stepped too far around the corner of the barn. A Red Delicious apple smashed into the side of my head. "Hey!" I shouted.

"That's enough out of you, LadyBugManGuy!"

Kira called from the roof of the barn. "You face the combined might of the . . . the Bug Brigade!" she yelled. Then a Fuji apple hit her in the stomach. "Oof!" she said as she stumbled backward.

"Kira!" I yelled.

Josie sped around to the other side of the barn. But even she couldn't catch Moth Girl before she fell into a nearby mountain of loose straw.

"Wait," said LadyBugManGuy. "Is she okay?"

I looked across the open grassy field. This LadyBugManGuy wasn't the typical supervillain we'd read about in Reginald's comic book collection. The man really did look like a giant ladybug, although he had a human head and stood on his back two feet. But he didn't seem that evil. Unless you counted his wheelbarrow of stolen lettuce. I squinted and examined his face.

"Whoa!" I said. "We know this guy!"

The ladybug look suddenly made complete sense. It was Professor Lad. The man in the white lab coat from the museum.

"We do?" said Kira as I pulled her out of the straw.

"I have a plan," I said. "Everyone, scatter!"

By the time LadyBugManGuy walked over to the side of the barn, the Bug Brigade (as Kira had apparently just named us) was nowhere to be seen. As it turned out, we insects were pretty good at scattering.

"Um, little butterfly person?" the would-be villain said, looking around. But all that stood in front of him was a pile of straw and a sticklike tree.

"She's a moth," said the tree.

LadyBugManGuy jumped in surprise. "Who said that?" he said.

"It wasn't me," said Josie in her deepest Captain Cockroach voice. She was now standing right next to LadyBugManGuy. He was so shocked, he dropped the last two apples he held in his hands. Then Josie zipped away behind the large mound of straw. The sort-of villain stumbled after her.

Suddenly LadyBugManGuy lost his balance completely. The "tree" had moved. Reginald had dove between the man's shins. LadyBugManGuy fell face-first into the pile of straw. He pulled himself out, only to see the "tree" standing in front of him again.

"How are you doing this?" he yelled.

"Moth Girl can't be defeated that easily!" said Kira. LadyBugManGuy looked up to see her perched on the top of the straw pile.

"I just wanted something leafy and delicious,"

said LadyBugManGuy. "I'm so hungry all the time."

"Then maybe you should pay for it rather than raiding every produce market in town," said the tree behind him.

LadyBugManGuy got to his feet. He tried to move away from the straw, but Captain Cockroach was standing in front of him. He turned and tried to head to his right, but Captain Cockroach again blocked his way.

"He's in position, Doug!" said Josie after zooming in front of LadyBugManGuy a third time.

Before LadyBugManGuy could react, I knocked him to the ground doing my best impression of an L-Bow foul. Using the straw, I rolled him across the lawn faster than even I thought I could. By the time he realized what was happening, LadyBugManGuy was trapped in a perfect roll of

tightly bound straw. He was now more burrito than supervillain.

"I think that wraps up this case!" I said. I immediately felt regret. Sure, I could blame it on being caught up in the moment. But really, there's never a good excuse for a pun that bad.

CHAPTER 7

I WAS TOLD THERE WOULD BE MORE CLAPPING

My palms were sweating. I couldn't make them stop. They'd been sweating when I had brushed my teeth at home that morning. They had been sweating through every single class at school that day.

And now that I was standing in line with my team at the school's Friday afternoon pep rally, my palms were sweating worse than ever.

I was finding it difficult to just hold on to my backpack without it slipping out of my hands and onto the floor.

". . . and we hope you have a great season!" Principal Duncan said. He looked at the team and clapped.

The audience sitting in the stands in the packed gymnasium clapped too.

I waited until the crowd quieted down. Then I stepped up to a nearby microphone stand. The audience was in the process of standing. They were ready to file out of the gym.

"Um, hello?" I said into the mic. I glanced out at all my classmates. They looked confused, then started to sit back down.

I took a deep breath. This was it. Time to stop living a lie. It was now or never.

"Um, I have an announcement to make," I said. "I've been keeping a secret from all of you."

I looked at Kira, Josie, and Reginald. They were seated in the front row of the bleachers. The looks on their faces said they had no idea what I was about to reveal.

"For over two years now, I've been part of a secret group of insect experts. We call ourselves the Bug Society of Littleton," I said.

I focused on Kira's face. She seemed as if she wasn't sure whether she wanted to smile or hide.

"But now, we've become something more. And I'm proud of who we are. I don't want to hide any longer."

I reached into my backpack and retrieved my black knit cap from it. I put it on. Then

I removed my sweatpants from the bag. I lost my balance a few times. Finally, I managed to tug them on over my shorts.

"We're the Bug Brigade," I said as I pulled my sweatshirt over my head.

Then I took the pose I'd been practicing in the mirror for the last week. "And I'm the Doug Beetle!" I said.

The audience was silent.

Then, slowly, they began to talk among themselves. They stood up and filed out of the gym.

It was like I hadn't just made my life's biggest confession.

No one was making fun of me. They didn't care about my superheroics one way or the other.

I stood behind the microphone until the entire place was empty, except for three people in the front row—Super Stick-Bug, Captain Cockroach, and Moth Girl.

All three were smiling from ear to ear.

"See?" said Reginald, as they walked over to me. "I told you that Doug Beetle is the perfect name."

I wiped my sweaty hands on my pants.

"Are you guys looking at the internet?" Josie said, holding her phone toward us. "People are saying a giant mealworm is raiding coolers at Mills River Camp. A giant mealworm, you guys." She was almost shaking. She could barely contain her excitement. "You know what that means!"

Then Josie sped out of the gym. Without missing a beat, we ran after her.

There was no doubt about it. This looked like a job for . . . well, for the park rangers.

But also for the Bug Brigade . . .

. . . probably?

GLOSSARY

elytra (EL-i-truh)—the wing cases of a beetle

entomologist (en-tuh-MOL-uh-jist)—a person who studies insects

indigenous (in-DIJ-uh-nuhs)—something found naturally in a particular place

origin (OR-i-jin)—the point of which something or someone begins

pilfer (PIL-fer)—to steal (usually things of little value)

pun (PUHN)—a joke based on one word that has two meanings or two words that sound the same but have different meanings

radioactive (ray-dee-oh-AK-tiv)—giving off or relating to radiation

unconscious (uhn-KAHN-shuhs)—not awake

DISCUSSION QUESTIONS

1. Do you think LadyBugManGuy was evil, misunderstood, or just really in need of a snack? Did the Bug Brigade handle his threat fairly?

2. How did Doug change during the course of the story? What will his relationship with his basketball team be like in the future?

3. How will the Bug Brigade's powers help their lives? How will those same powers hurt their lives? Will Doug ever eat a healthy meal again?

WRITING PROMPTS

1. If you had to be gifted/cursed with the powers of an insect, what insect would you choose? Write a paragraph describing your amazing (or extremely silly) abilities.

2. Write and draw the next adventure of your favorite member of the Bug Brigade in a one-page comic. Be sure to use both words and pictures to tell your tale!

3. What was LadyBugManGuy thinking during all the crazy action at the farmers' market? Write a paragraph telling the story from his point of view.

ABOUT THE AUTHOR

The author of the Amazon best-selling hardcover *Batman: A Visual History*, MATTHEW K. MANNING has contributed to many comic books, including Beware the Batman, Spider-Man Unlimited, Pirates of the Caribbean: Six Sea Shanties, Justice League Adventures, Looney Tunes, and Scooby-Doo, Where Are You? He currently resides in Asheville, North Carolina, with his wife, Dorothy, and their two daughters, Lillian and Gwendolyn.

ABOUT THE ILLUSTRATOR

ETHEN BEAVERS lives in Central California and has been working in children's books, comics, and animation for over ten years. He is a big fan of Star and Samurai Jack, as well as fly-fishing for trout ac ern U.S.

JOKING AROUND

What do you call a fly with no wings?
A walk!

How do bees get to school?
On the school buzz!

What bug is on the ground and also a hundred feet
in the air?
A centipede on its back!

Why didn't the butterfly go to the school dance?
Because it was a moth ball!

Why was the dung beetle late for the party?
It was on duty!

Did you hear about the two silkworms that ran in a race?
They ended in a tie!

Luna-ticks!

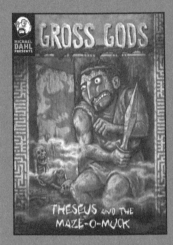